P9-DUD-554

A Kite for Melia

Samuel Narh and Freda Narh

Illustrated by Valeria Suria

Melia watches the older
kids fly kites over a ridge.
She wants to fly one, too.

She misses Ginger and how
they chased fireflies up and
down the hills.

Melia asks the older kids,
"Can I also play with your kites?"
In unison, they say,
"Go and make your own kite!"

Melia doesn't know how to make a kite.
These kids won't teach her, either.
She wishes that their kites would get
stuck in a baobab tree.

Melia knows that some of the smartest people
visit the library on the other side of town.
She's played with Ginger in the fields of the library.
Maybe one of them can assist her.

With twists and
turns, these dusty
roads seem endless.
Even so, the sight of
the library fills her
heart with joy.

But no one here knows how to make a kite.
Melia feels like throwing away the items for her kite.

Somehow, she suspects that an answer is close by.
She finds a book about kites hidden in a case.
She discovers twinkles of beauty in silence;
this aged booklet smells like success.

She makes a kite with a bow on its tail.

Melia goes back
to the ridge.
Her kite won't fly.

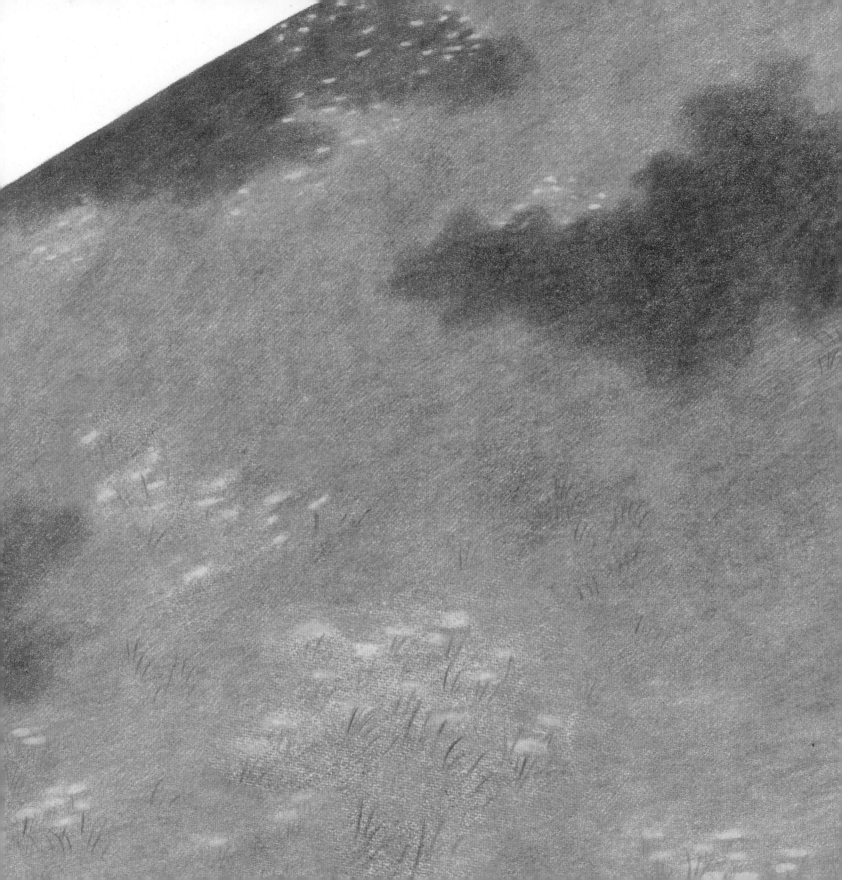

The older kids tease
her in unison,
"A pig with a bow
still won't fly."
Tears fill her eyes as
she tries again.

Her kite circles in the air like
a dog chasing its tail.
They laugh at her, frightening
a stubborn fawn nearby.

"My kite is an eagle,"
she whispers to herself.
She centers the bridle of her kite.
The older kids are speechless now.
Melia's kite dances with a rainbow.

Her kite tugs, feeling heavy, as it soars into the cradle of the sky. Melia's face beams with joy, because she's tagged a note on her kite for Ginger.

Perhaps her best
friend might also
hang a note for
Melia on a star.

Melia feels her heart
soar like the kite.
She knows that Ginger
is happy chasing
fireflies in the sky.